First published in 2017 by Nosy Crow Ltd
The Crow's Nest, 10a Lant Street
London SE1 1QR
www.nosycrow.com

ISBN 978 0 85763 887 8 (HB)
ISBN 978 0 85763 888 5 (PB)

Nosy Crow and associated logos are trademarks and/or
registered trademarks of Nosy Crow Ltd.

Text and illustrations © Hrefna Bragadottir 2017

The right of Hrefna Bragadottir to be identified as the author
and illustrator of this work has been asserted.

A CIP catalogue record for this book is available from the British Library.

Printed in China

Papers used by Nosy Crow are made from
wood grown in sustainable forests.

10 9 8 7 6 5 4 3 2 1 (HB)
10 9 8 7 6 5 4 3 2 1 (PB)

FOR: RYAN ARNAR

Noodles

FRUIT & VEG

STEVE

Harvey the HERO

Hrefna Bragadottir

I'm Harvey
and today is a **big** day for me.

Superhero Steve is in town
telling us **all** about his job.

Steve's a **real** hero. Every day he's so busy.

He stops thieves . . .

He puts out fires . . .

and he saves lives.

Wow! I wish I was
a **hero**, too.

But wait!
Oh no!
Steve's left his
cape behind.

I'd better follow him to the Big City
right now!

Gulp. The Big City is so busy!
How am I ever going to find Steve?

I bet heroes **always** know their way around.

Still, maybe I can find someone to help me.

Ah, look!
A map! That's just what I need.
Thank you!

Let's see. Steve's house must be . . . **this** way . . .

... I think.
But – oh dear – I've been reading the map upside down.
Whoops! I bet heroes don't do that!

Now, I'm sure **this** is the right way to Steve's house.
I hope it's not far.

But wait!
My stomach is **rumbling**.
I must have missed lunch!

Yum! This sandwich is SO delicious . . .

Silly me! I bet heroes don't forget to eat their lunch.

Right, off I go **again**.

Steve's house must be just
around the next corner . . .

. . . or maybe not.

It can't be far now, but I've
been walking for **hours**!

Finding Steve is
hard work!

Maybe I'll sit down,
just for a minute.

Oh, it's good to have a little rest.

But I'd better get going.
After all, I bet heroes don't stop for a nap.

At last! I've made it to Steve's house.

Through the park . . .

past the cafe . . .

into the station . . .

There's no place like home . . .

but I wonder why everyone is so pleased to see me?

What's that? I'm on TV?!
Are they talking about ... me?

Who would have thought it?
It turns out . . .

. . . I'm Harvey the Hero!